The Adventures of Plush and Tatty

by Molly Brett

© THE MEDICI SOCIETY LTD · LONDON 1985. Printed in England. B79. ISBN 0 85503 079 8

TWO BEARS IN A BOAT

Tatty, the little teddy bear, ran down to the stream to see what her friend Plush was doing.

Tatty was small and quiet and her fur coat was rather worn in places, but Plush was a grand bear with lovely golden fur and he wore a different coloured ribbon every day, so Tatty was very proud to have him as her friend.

Plush was busy painting a little boat, 'Come along Tatty,' he growled, 'we are off tomorrow on a trip down the river and — don't be late.' 'What? me too!' squeaked the delighted Tatty, 'Oh Plush how lovely! and can I help paint the boat?' 'You would not know how,' growled her friend, 'but you can hold the paint pot.'

As Plush added the last touches a fly settled on the wet paint, 'Go away!' bawled the bear slapping at it with his paws and spilling all the paint. 'No more paint — except on *you*,' remarked Tatty, while Plush muttered, 'I'll have to change my ribbon,' as his friend ran off to prepare for their trip.

Next morning they pushed the little boat into the stream and Plush growled, 'Now, Tatty, stand by to untie the rope while I get out the oars,' and Tatty waited on the bank while Plush settled himself in the boat and bawled impatiently, 'Hop aboard, Tatty, or we'll miss the tide.' There was not any tide but he thought it sounded important.

'But what about . . .' began Tatty when Plush interrupted her by growling, 'Hurry up, or I'll go without you.' So she skipped into the boat, but, though Plush splashed about with the oars, they did not move from the shore.

Then Tatty squeaked meekly, 'Perhaps the boat would go faster if the rope you told me to untie was not still tied up on the bank!' So the rope was unfastened, but Plush was not very good at steering and presently — BUMP! — the boat ran into the bank. The bears pushed it off with the oars but when Plush looked round — Tatty wasn't there! She was still clinging to her oar which had stuck in the mud.

Safely back in the boat the teddy bears floated on very happily until Tatty squeaked, 'I can hear a roaring sound!' But Plush replied, 'Only the wind in the trees,' and then round a bend in the stream was . . . a WATERFALL!

The current was running fast now and the little boat was swept along to the brink of the rushing water and, just in time, Plush and Tatty seized an overhanging branch and held on to it.

'Trust *me* not to get wet!' chuckled Plush as they set off to look for the boat which had gone over the fall. It was floating quite near the bank and Plush growled, 'See me jump aboard!' — but next moment — SPLOSH! The boat moved away and left poor Plush floundering in the water.

'What a pity you are so wet,' squeaked Tatty,' after being high and dry on the branch.' Then, as the oars were lost, they tied up the boat and started on the long walk home.

PLUSH GIVES A PARTY

One early summer morning Plush called on his friend Tatty with a wonderful idea. 'I am planning a grand May Day Party,' he explained, 'I shall be Master of the Ceremonies and there will be dancing round the maypole, and the party will end with a wonderful surprise — which is a secret.' So the two bears were very busy putting up the maypole, practising on their fiddles so that there would be music for the dancing, and preparing a lovely tea.

Then on May Day all the little bears from Teddy Bear Town and their parents arrived for the party, with Plush pushing them into position round the maypole, ribbons held tightly in their paws, while he and Tatty started to play their fiddles and the bears skipped round the maypole.

'You are not keeping time, now do please dance properly . . . *I'll* show you,' bawled Plush pushing in among the dancers, but the little bears started to skip round Plush until he was all tied up in the ribbons and it took a long time to disentangle him.

Tatty was told to make the tea, and refreshments were handed round. Meanwhile Plush disappeared to produce his Grand Secret Surprise.

A surprise it certainly was for after a long pause what should appear overhead but a — BALLOON — with Plush high in the air scattering sweeties for the little bears below.

How everyone cheered until the balloon floated too close to a prickly bush and POP! it was pierced by the thorns, and poor Plush descended very rapidly into a clump of sticky green Goose Grass.

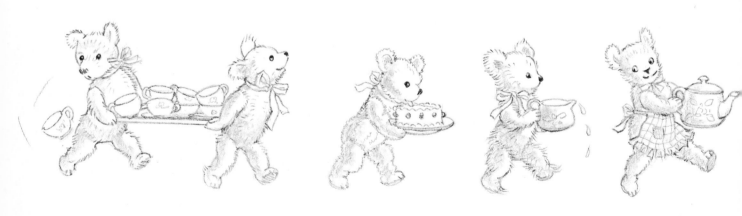

Nothing could be seen of him but presently a strange green object emerged, waving its arms and growling loudly. It advanced on the party, frightening the little bears so much that they started to run away squeaking, 'It must be a Dragon! It will gobble us up!' while their parents started in pursuit to comfort them.

Soon none of the May Day Party was left except Plush and Tatty. 'You turned out to be a Jack-in-the-green instead of Master of the Ceremonies,' squeaked Tatty pulling all the sticky weed off poor Plush, but perhaps you thought that TWO surprises would be better than one!'

TWO BEARS AND A BARBECUE

'Autumn will soon be here, so we must hurry up and have a barbecue,' growled Plush to his friend Tatty. The two teddy bears were soon very busy sending out invitations to their friends in Teddy Bear Town, and buying sausages and beefburgers, so that everything was ready for the barbecue on a fine evening with bears hurrying to join the party.

Tatty scuttled around with the beefburgers and hung a string of sausages on a low branch under a tree, while Plush was busy lighting a fire for the cooking to begin. It did not burn very well, so Plush started to puff and blow until the flames flickered and glowed in the twilight.

Just then Tatty caught sight of the sausages — FLYING OFF OVER HER HEAD! In astonishment she dropped the beefburgers she was carrying, so that they fell off the plate, and gave chase.

The string of sausages was now dangling from a nearby tree and Old Mr Owl held the other end in his beak. 'I like sausages,' he hooted and 'Hiccup!' added Mr Owl as he gobbled up the sausages much too fast. Meanwhile Plush had got the fire burning brightly, 'Phew!' he sighed, 'all that blowing has made me quite out-of-breath,' and he flopped down on a tree stump to rest.

Up came Tatty in tears. 'Oh Plush,' she sobbed, 'that old Owl has eaten all the sausages!' 'Never mind,' comforted Plush, 'you cook the beefburgers and I'll roast some potatoes.'

Now *where* did I put them?' squeaked Tatty but . . . the beefburgers had disappeared! Then Plush got up from the stump on which he had been sitting and turned to roast the potatoes and . . . there were the beefburgers — but they were very flat indeed after being sat on by Plush. 'No one will notice when they are cooked,' he growled and went to greet their guests while Tatty was not pleased to see that Polly Polar Bear had arrived; she had a lovely white fur coat and gave herself airs.

'How careless of Tatty to lose the sausages!' she giggled. This made Tatty very cross as she poked up the fire, wishing she could poke Polly too; the flames shot up — PUFF! — the beefburgers caught fire and black smoke covered everybody.

The bears had to brush the smuts out of their fur coats and Plush growled, 'Its a blackout for beefburgers — but we still have the potatoes. Meanwhile Polly Polar Bear complained, 'What a horrid barbecue! I must have a bath,' which made Tatty whisper to Plush, 'What a grizzly bear, perhaps she will shrink in the wash!' Then all the teddy bears enjoyed the roast potatoes.

TWO BEARS AND THE SNOWMAN

It was a cold winter day when Tatty and Plush decided to make a snowman. They set off carrying a broom and a spade and were soon hard at work with Plush giving orders and instructions, while Tatty scuttled around putting finishing touches to a very fine snowman.

'Now Tatty,' growled Plush, standing back to admire their work, 'you have forgotten to give him any buttons down his front.' So Tatty found some stones to serve as buttons. 'Really, Tatty,' growled Plush, 'you have not given him any feet.' So Tatty swept up more snow as ordered. 'We need a snowball now to make him a nose,' growled Plush, 'just a *little* more snow, Tatty, and he'll be the very finest snowman to be seen,' and he waved his spade in the air with pride.

Next moment a big lump of snow was knocked off an overhanging branch by the spade and — PLONK! — it fell on Plush followed by more and more. Tatty stood and stared in amazement — where there had been *one* snowman there were now *two!*

'Oh Plush,' she giggled brushing all the snow off her friend, 'that "little bit of snow" turned out to be rather a lot!'

Plush did not like being turned into a snowman and when he had shaken the snow out of his ears and eyes he suggested they should go skating on the pond, which was quite crowded with big and little teddy bears.

Tatty and Plush glided about in fine style and then Plush started to show off. He whirled Tatty around at such a pace that she was quite giddy, and dashed in and out among the other bears until suddenly Tatty squealed, 'STOP!' please stop — I have dropped a stitch!'

Now Tatty had knitted herself a little woolly jersey, but she was not very good at knitting and a strand of wool had become undone, so more and more stitches were being unravelled and the wool was becoming wound round the other bears as Plush dashed about among them.

Soon everyone was in a tangle with poor Tatty trying to unwind the wool from legs and paws. Then, clutching the ball of wool, she scuttled home and spent the rest of the day knitting to replace her little woolly jersey.

'I don't like skating,' squeaked Tatty, 'I think I have caught a cold losing half my woolly jersey — Atishoo!' 'And *I* don't like snowmen,' growled Plush, 'and I think *I* have caught a cold getting covered in snow — ATISHOO!'

Then they both sneezed together — A T I S H O O !